SO-AGE-293

RED ROOM ESCAPEE. HANK PYM'S DAUGHTER. SUPER-SCIENCING FOR GOOD. NADIA IS...

THE UNSTOPPABLE WASP

UNSTOPPABLE! #3

NADIA HAS A NEW MISSION: TO RECRUIT FEMALE GENIUSES TO HER LAB AND USE THEIR COMBINED KNOWLEDGE TO CHANGE THE WORLD FOR THE BETTER. BUT WHEN SHE TRIED TO RECRUIT KID GENIUS LUNELLA LAFAYETTE, A.K.A. MOON GIRL, THEY WERE BOTH ATTACKED BY A PYM-PARTICLE-ENLARGED RAT! NADIA TRACED THE RAT BACK TO THE PERSON CONTROLLING IT...WHO TURNED OUT TO BE RED ROOM ASSASSIN AND NADIA'S FORMER LAB PARTNER, YING!

writer
JEREMY WHITLEY

artist
ELSA CHARRETIER

color artist
MEGAN WILSON

letterer
VC'S JOE CARAMAGNA

cover
ELSA CHARRETIER & NICOLAS BANNISTER

variant cover
PAULINA GANUCHEAU

editors
ALANNA SMITH & TOM BREVOORT

editor in chief
AXEL ALONSO

chief creative officer
JOE QUESADA

publisher
DAN BUCKLEY

executive producer
ALAN FINE

SPECIAL THANKS TO PREETI CHHIBBER

WASP CREATED BY STAN LEE, ERNIE HART AND JACK KIRBY

MARVEL · ABDO Spotlight

ABDOBOOKS.COM

Reinforced library bound edition published in 2020 by Spotlight,
a division of ABDO, PO Box 398166, Minneapolis, Minnesota 55439.
Spotlight produces high-quality reinforced library bound editions for
schools and libraries. Published by agreement with Marvel Characters, Inc.

Printed in the United States of America, North Mankato, Minnesota.
042019
092019

marvelkids.com
© 2020 MARVEL

Library of Congress Control Number: 2018965979

Publisher's Cataloging-in-Publication Data

Names: Whitley, Jeremy, author. | Charretier, Elsa; Wilson, Megan, illustrators.
Title: Unstoppable! / writer: Jeremy Whitley; art: Elsa Charretier; Megan Wilson.
Description: Minneapolis, Minnesota : Spotlight, 2020 | Series: The unstoppable
    Wasp
Summary: Nadia Pym spreads her wings as she recruits girl geniuses of the Marvel
    universe, battles evil scientists and man-eating rats, and avoids the Red Room's
    clutches.
Identifiers: ISBN 9781532143656 (#1 ; lib. bdg.) | ISBN 9781532143663 (#2 ; lib.
    bdg.) | ISBN 9781532143670 (#3 ; lib. bdg.) | ISBN 9781532143687 (#4 ; lib.
    bdg.)
Subjects: LCSH: Wasp (Fictitious character)--Juvenile fiction. | Superheroes--Juvenile
    fiction. | Women superheroes--Juvenile fiction. | Graphic novels--Juvenile
    fiction. | Geniuses--Juvenile fiction. | Superpowers--Juvenile fiction. | Comic
    books, strips, etc--Juvenile fiction.
Classification: DDC 741.5--dc23

Spotlight

A Division of ABDO
abdobooks.com

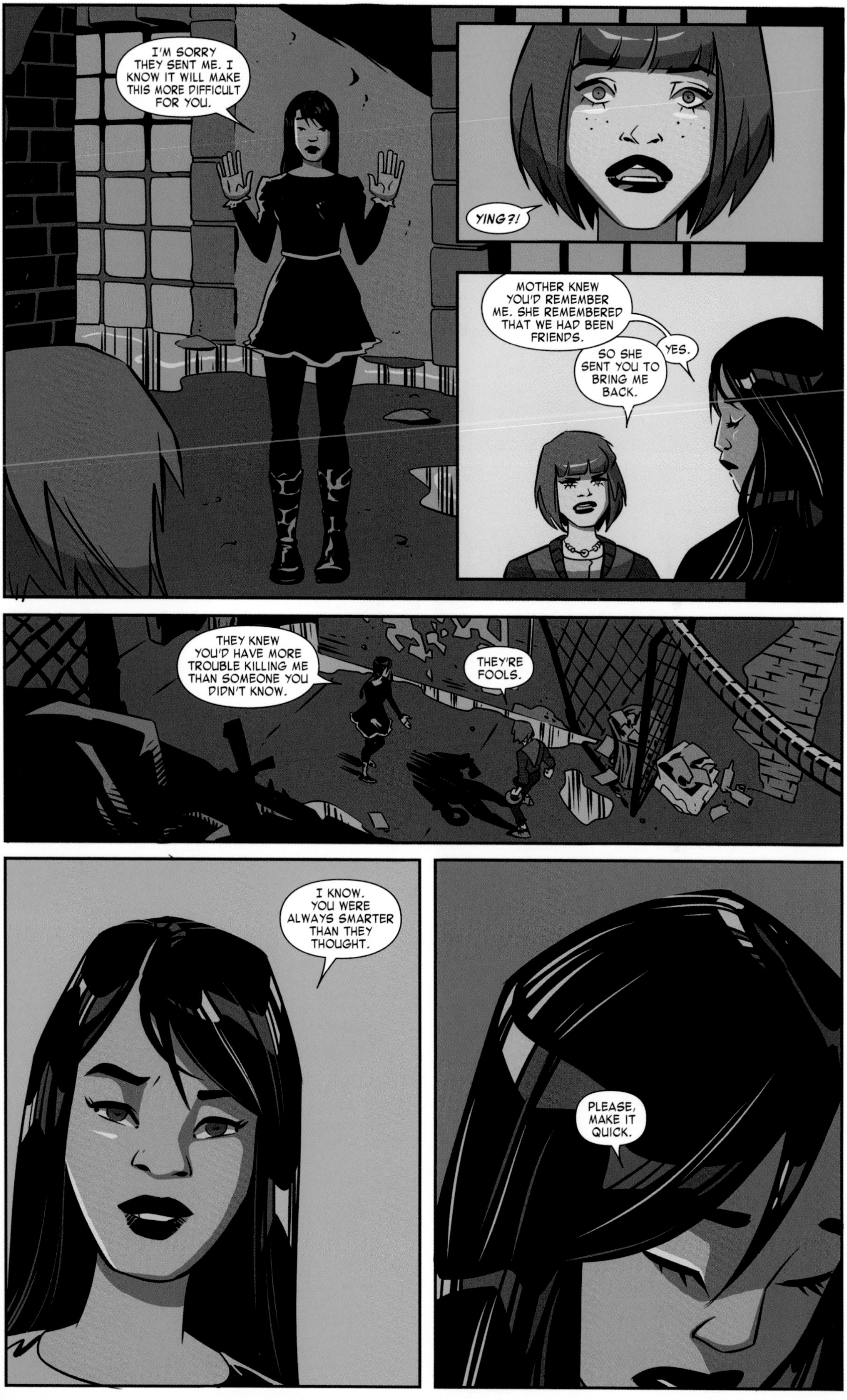
I'M SORRY THEY SENT ME. I KNOW IT WILL MAKE THIS MORE DIFFICULT FOR YOU.
YING?!
MOTHER KNEW YOU'D REMEMBER ME. SHE REMEMBERED THAT WE HAD BEEN FRIENDS.
YES.
SO SHE SENT YOU TO BRING ME BACK.
THEY KNEW YOU'D HAVE MORE TROUBLE KILLING ME THAN SOMEONE YOU DIDN'T KNOW.
THEY'RE FOOLS.
I KNOW. YOU WERE ALWAYS SMARTER THAN THEY THOUGHT.
PLEASE, MAKE IT QUICK.

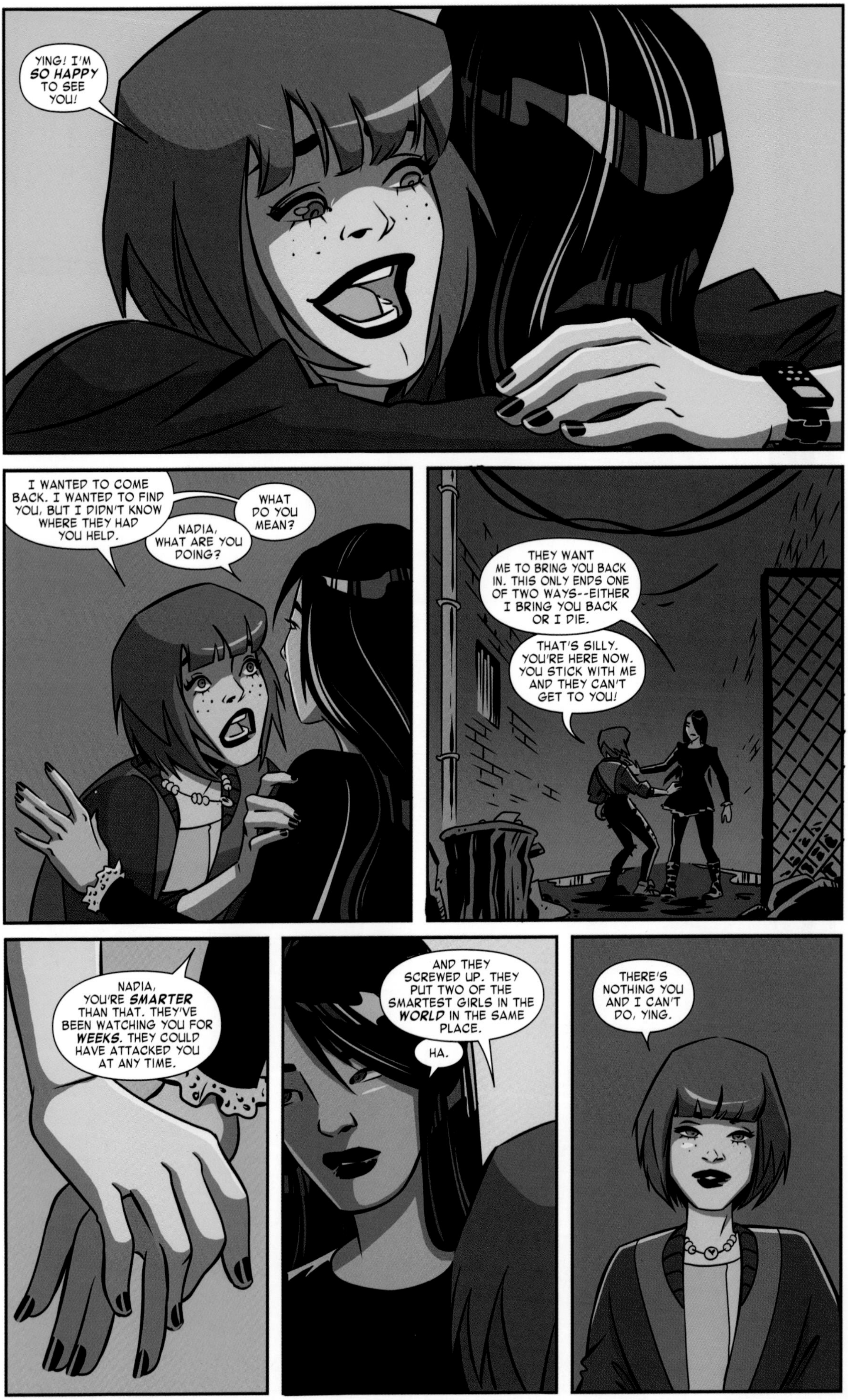

YING! I'M SO HAPPY TO SEE YOU!
I WANTED TO COME BACK. I WANTED TO FIND YOU, BUT I DIDN'T KNOW WHERE THEY HAD YOU HELD.
NADIA, WHAT ARE YOU DOING?
WHAT DO YOU MEAN?
THEY WANT ME TO BRING YOU BACK IN. THIS ONLY ENDS ONE OF TWO WAYS--EITHER I BRING YOU BACK OR I DIE.
THAT'S SILLY. YOU'RE HERE NOW. YOU STICK WITH ME AND THEY CAN'T GET TO YOU!
NADIA, YOU'RE SMARTER THAN THAT. THEY'VE BEEN WATCHING YOU FOR WEEKS. THEY COULD HAVE ATTACKED YOU AT ANY TIME.
AND THEY SCREWED UP. THEY PUT TWO OF THE SMARTEST GIRLS IN THE WORLD IN THE SAME PLACE.
HA.
THERE'S NOTHING YOU AND I CAN'T DO, YING.

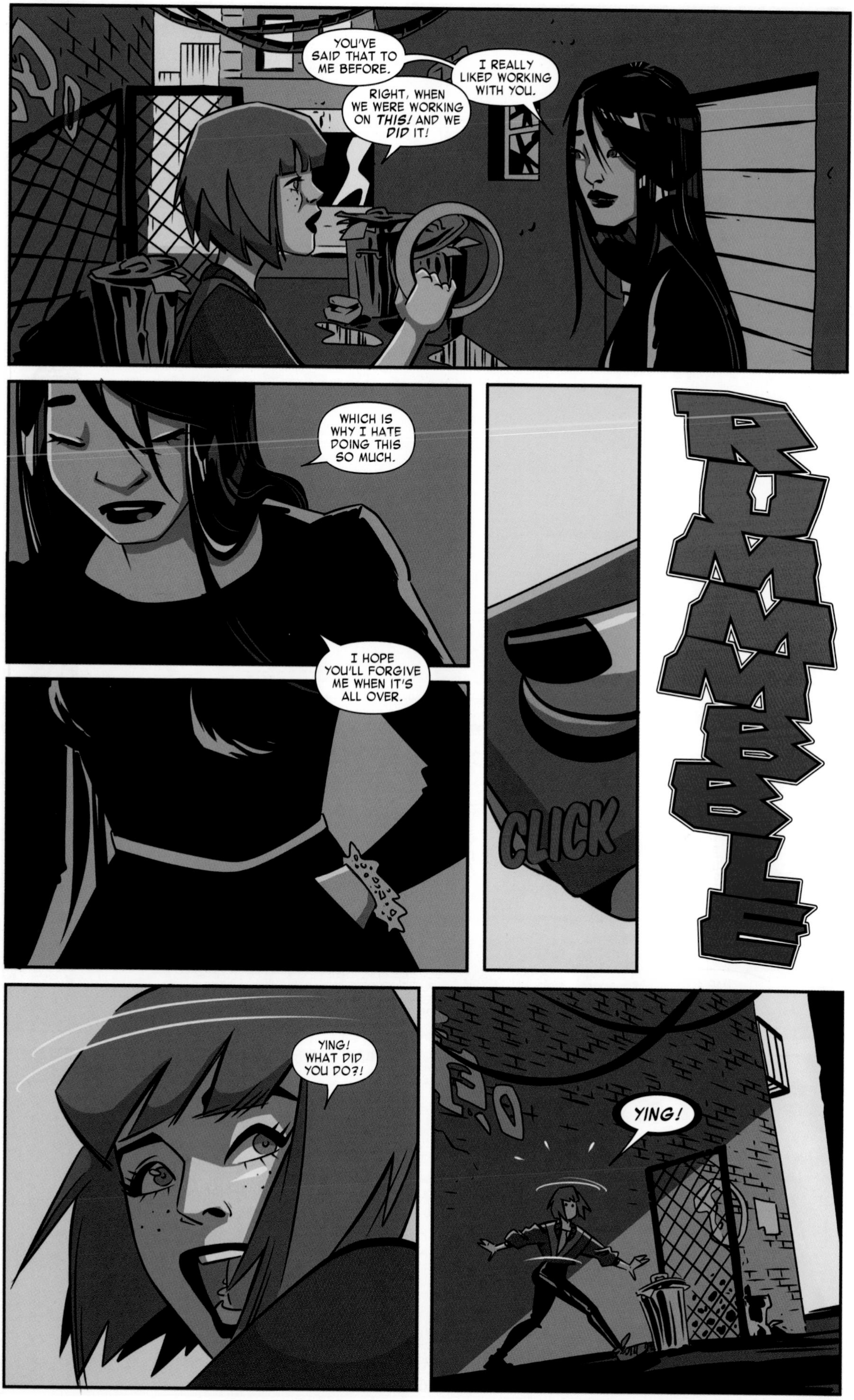
I REALLY LIKED WORKING WITH YOU.
YOU'VE SAID THAT TO ME BEFORE.
RIGHT, WHEN WE WERE WORKING ON THIS! AND WE DID IT!
WHICH IS WHY I HATE DOING THIS SO MUCH.
I HOPE YOU'LL FORGIVE ME WHEN IT'S ALL OVER.
CLICK
RUMMMBBLE
YING! WHAT DID YOU DO?!
YING!

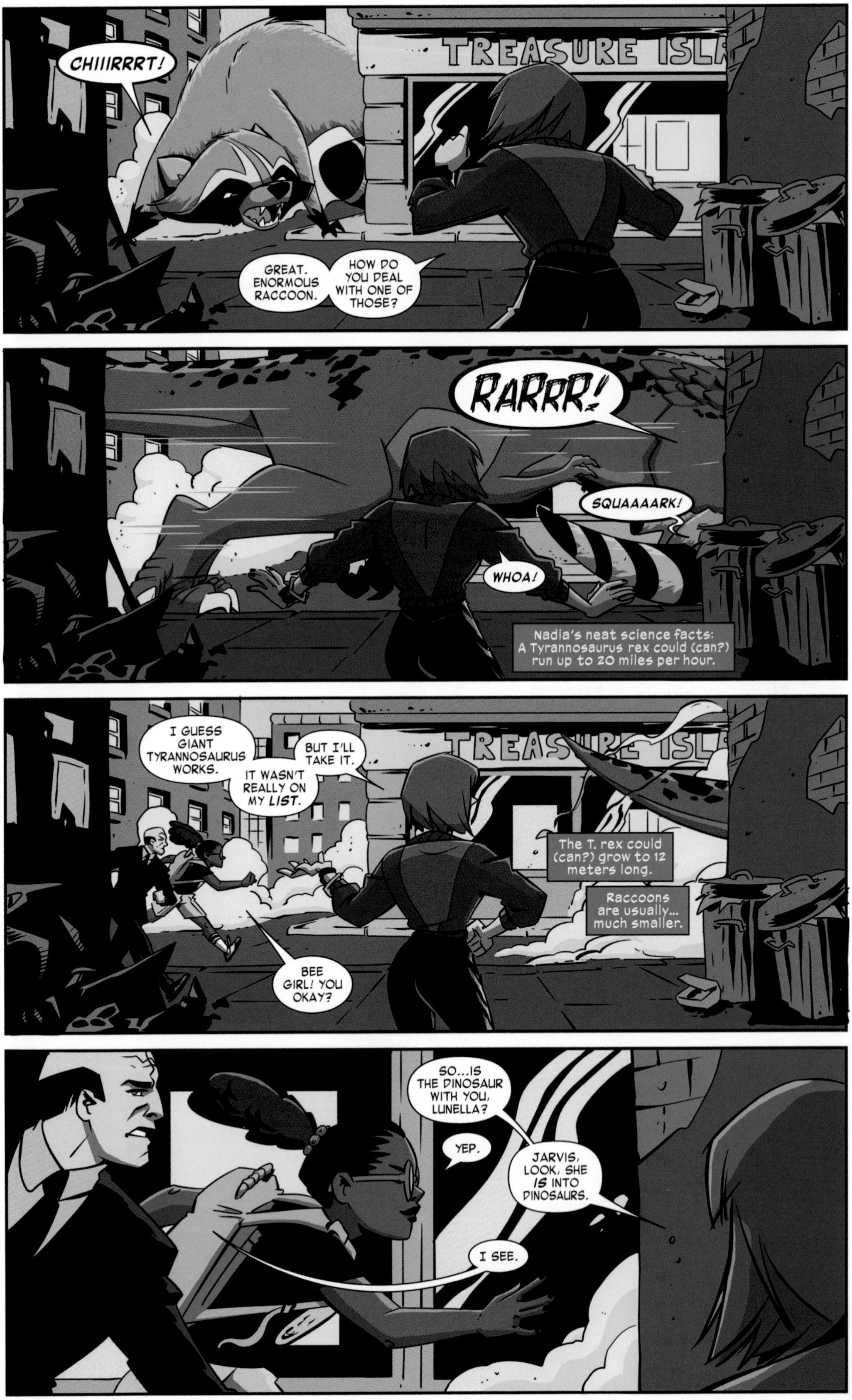
CHIIIRRRT!
TREASURE ISLA
GREAT. ENORMOUS RACCOON.
HOW DO YOU DEAL WITH ONE OF THOSE?
RARRR!
SQUAAAARK!
WHOA!
Nadia's neat science facts: A Tyrannosaurus rex could (can?) run up to 20 miles per hour.
TREASURE ISLA
I GUESS GIANT TYRANNOSAURUS WORKS.
IT WASN'T REALLY ON MY LIST.
BUT I'LL TAKE IT.
The T. rex could (can?) grow to 12 meters long.
Raccoons are usually... much smaller.
BEE GIRL! YOU OKAY?
SO...IS THE DINOSAUR WITH YOU, LUNELLA?
YEP.
JARVIS, LOOK, SHE IS INTO DINOSAURS.
I SEE.

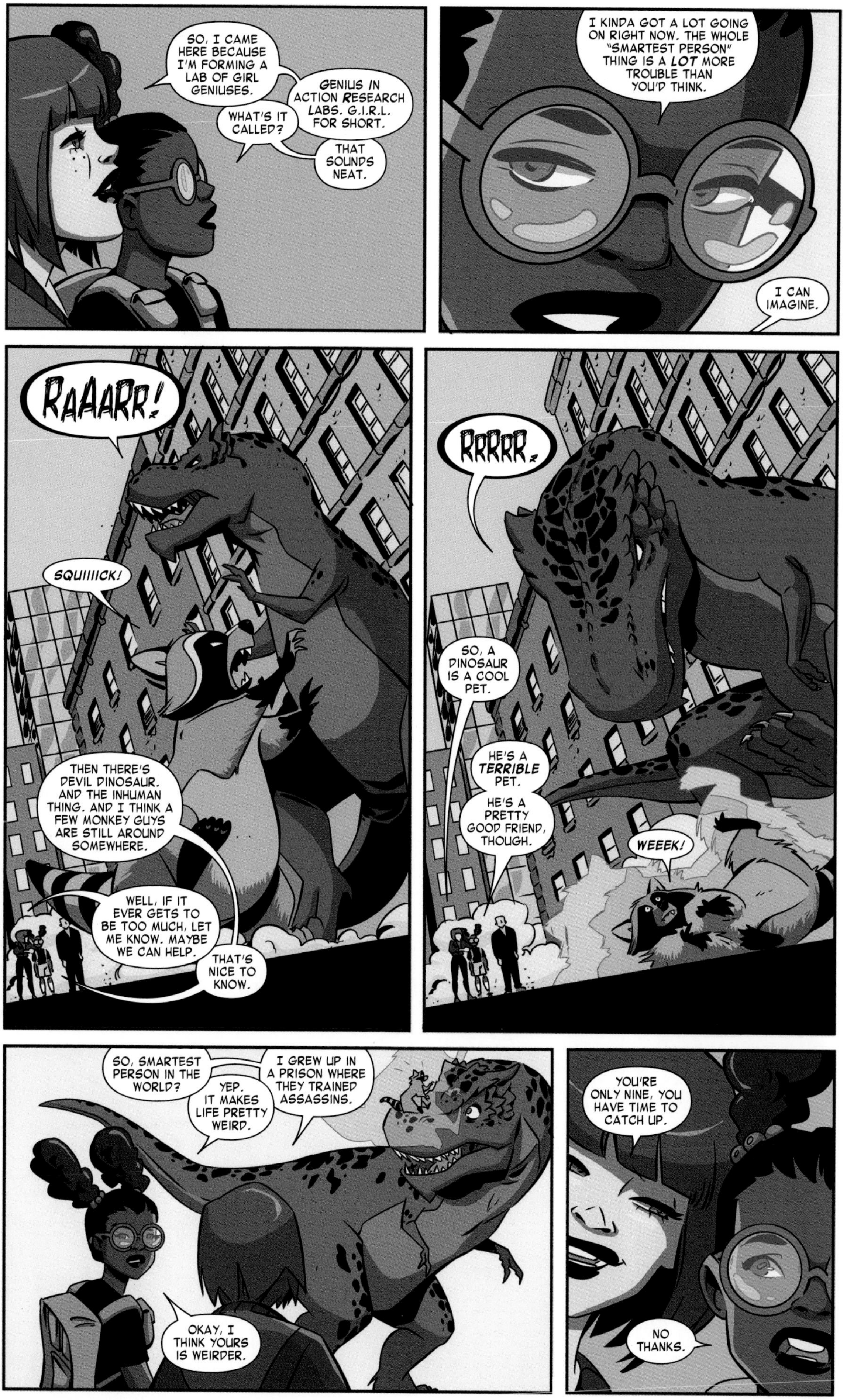
SO, I CAME HERE BECAUSE I'M FORMING A LAB OF GIRL GENIUSES.
WHAT'S IT CALLED?
GENIUS IN ACTION RESEARCH LABS. G.I.R.L. FOR SHORT.
THAT SOUNDS NEAT.
I KINDA GOT A LOT GOING ON RIGHT NOW. THE WHOLE "SMARTEST PERSON" THING IS A LOT MORE TROUBLE THAN YOU'D THINK.
I CAN IMAGINE.
RAAARR!
SQUIIIICK!
THEN THERE'S DEVIL DINOSAUR. AND THE INHUMAN THING. AND I THINK A FEW MONKEY GUYS ARE STILL AROUND SOMEWHERE.
WELL, IF IT EVER GETS TO BE TOO MUCH, LET ME KNOW. MAYBE WE CAN HELP.
THAT'S NICE TO KNOW.
RRRRR.
SO, A DINOSAUR IS A COOL PET.
HE'S A TERRIBLE PET.
HE'S A PRETTY GOOD FRIEND, THOUGH.
WEEEK!
SO, SMARTEST PERSON IN THE WORLD?
YEP. IT MAKES LIFE PRETTY WEIRD.
I GREW UP IN A PRISON WHERE THEY TRAINED ASSASSINS.
OKAY, I THINK YOURS IS WEIRDER.
YOU'RE ONLY NINE, YOU HAVE TIME TO CATCH UP.
NO THANKS.

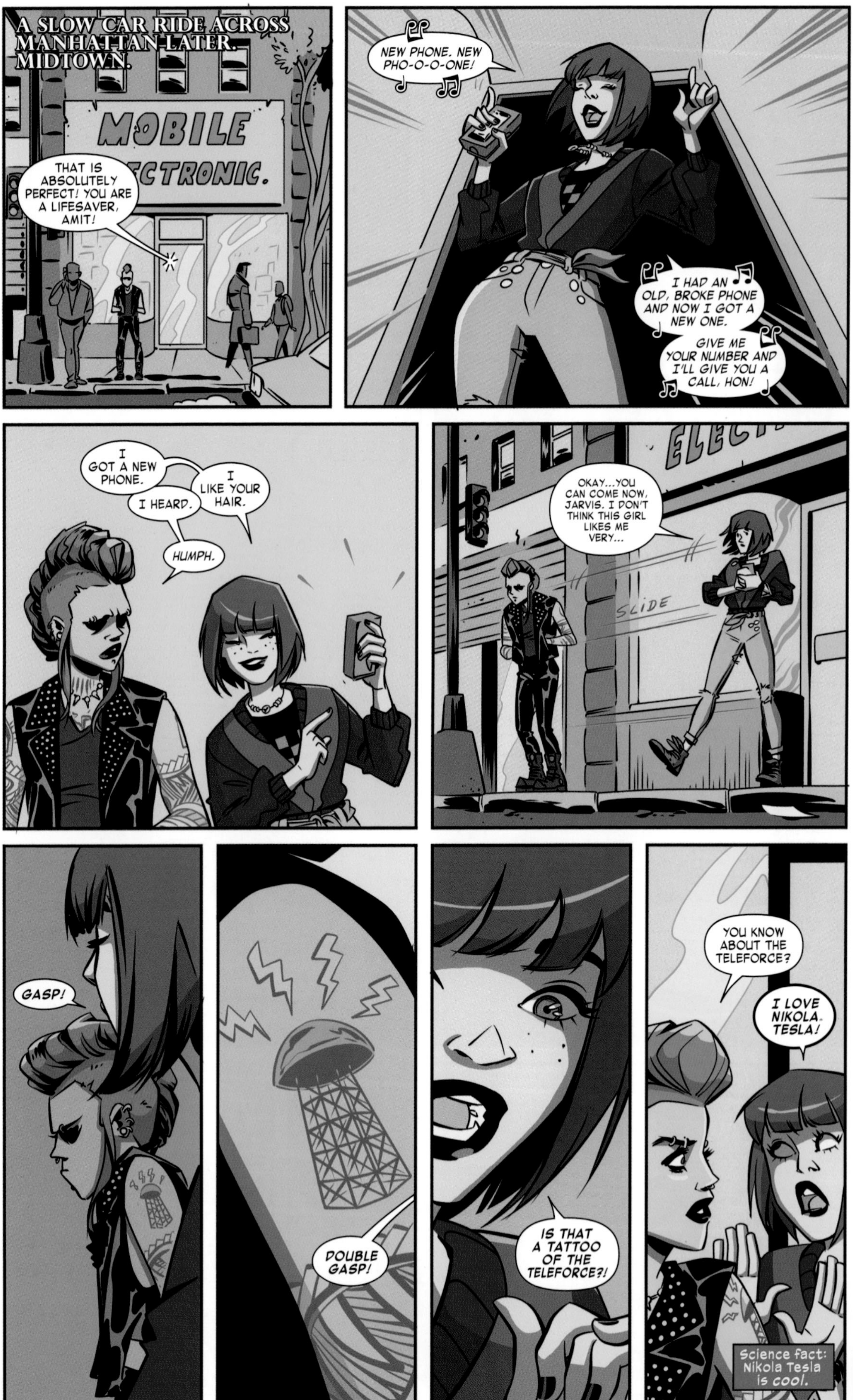

A SLOW CAR RIDE ACROSS MANHATTAN LATER. MIDTOWN.
MOBILE
ECTRONIC.
THAT IS ABSOLUTELY PERFECT! YOU ARE A LIFESAVER, AMIT!
NEW PHONE. NEW PHO-O-O-ONE!
I HAD AN OLD, BROKE PHONE AND NOW I GOT A NEW ONE.
GIVE ME YOUR NUMBER AND I'LL GIVE YOU A CALL, HON!
I GOT A NEW PHONE.
I HEARD.
I LIKE YOUR HAIR.
HUMPH.
ELEC
OKAY...YOU CAN COME NOW, JARVIS. I DON'T THINK THIS GIRL LIKES ME VERY...
SLIDE
GASP!
DOUBLE GASP!
IS THAT A TATTOO OF THE TELEFORCE?!
YOU KNOW ABOUT THE TELEFORCE?
I LOVE NIKOLA TESLA!
Science fact: Nikola Tesla is cool.

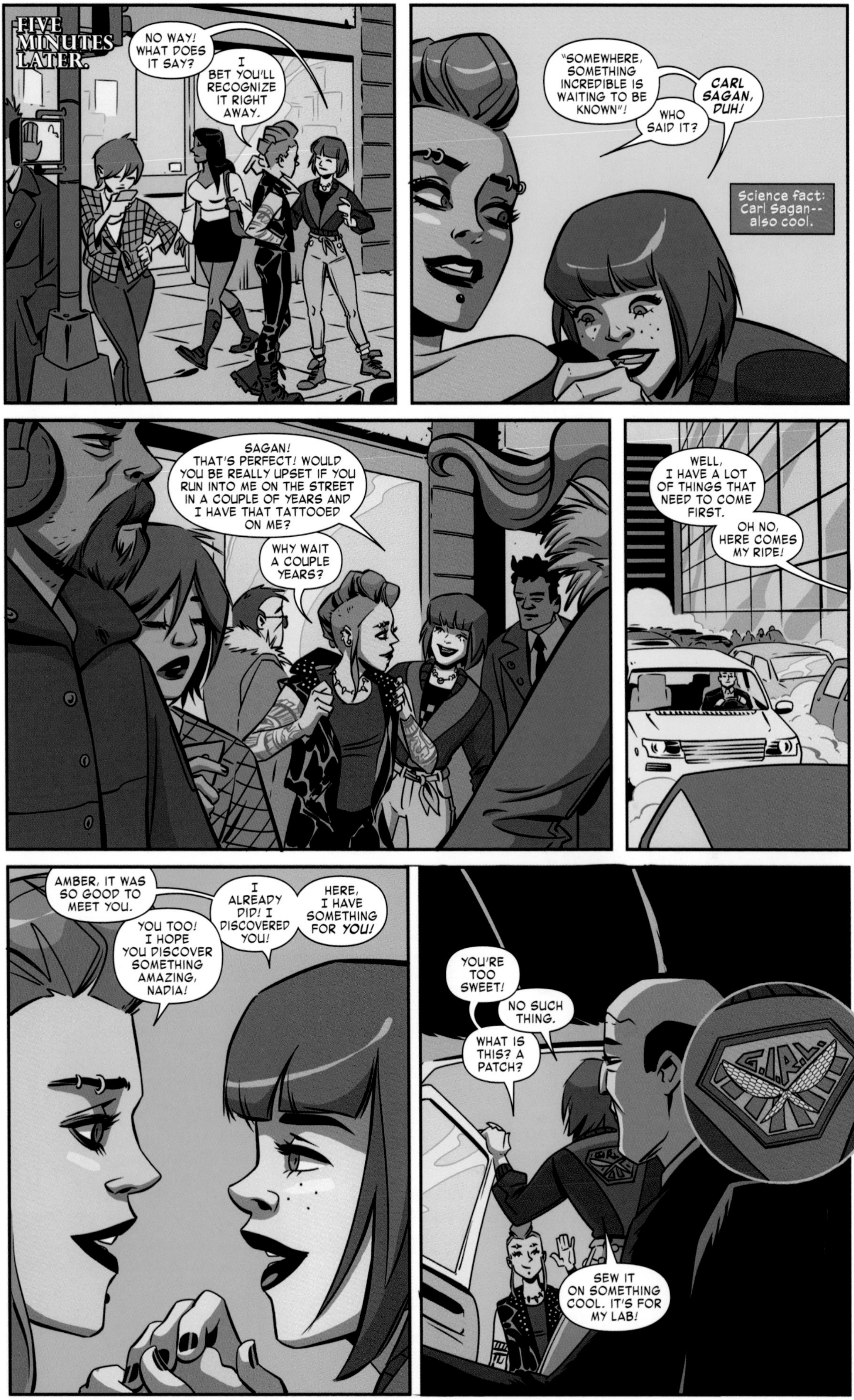
FIVE MINUTES LATER.
NO WAY! WHAT DOES IT SAY?
I BET YOU'LL RECOGNIZE IT RIGHT AWAY.
"SOMEWHERE, SOMETHING INCREDIBLE IS WAITING TO BE KNOWN"!
WHO SAID IT?
CARL SAGAN, DUH!
Science fact: Carl Sagan-- also cool.
SAGAN! THAT'S PERFECT! WOULD YOU BE REALLY UPSET IF YOU RUN INTO ME ON THE STREET IN A COUPLE OF YEARS AND I HAVE THAT TATTOOED ON ME?
WHY WAIT A COUPLE YEARS?
WELL, I HAVE A LOT OF THINGS THAT NEED TO COME FIRST.
OH NO, HERE COMES MY RIDE!
AMBER, IT WAS SO GOOD TO MEET YOU.
YOU TOO! I HOPE YOU DISCOVER SOMETHING AMAZING, NADIA!
I ALREADY DID! I DISCOVERED YOU!
HERE, I HAVE SOMETHING FOR YOU!
YOU'RE TOO SWEET!
NO SUCH THING.
WHAT IS THIS? A PATCH?
SEW IT ON SOMETHING COOL. IT'S FOR MY LAB!

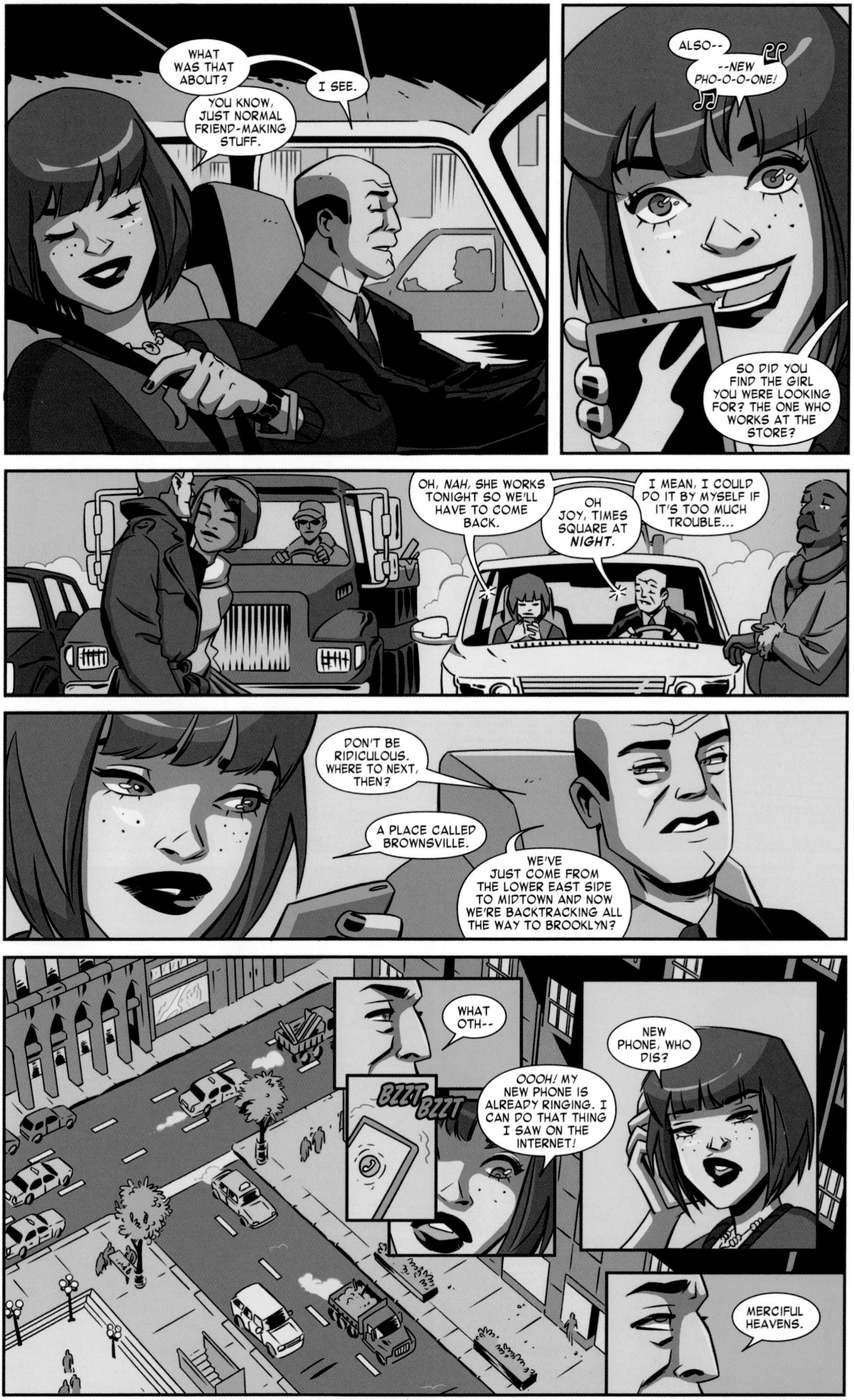
WHAT WAS THAT ABOUT?
YOU KNOW, JUST NORMAL FRIEND-MAKING STUFF.
I SEE.
ALSO--
--NEW PHO-O-O-ONE!
SO DID YOU FIND THE GIRL YOU WERE LOOKING FOR? THE ONE WHO WORKS AT THE STORE?
OH, NAH, SHE WORKS TONIGHT SO WE'LL HAVE TO COME BACK.
OH JOY, TIMES SQUARE AT NIGHT.
I MEAN, I COULD DO IT BY MYSELF IF IT'S TOO MUCH TROUBLE...
DON'T BE RIDICULOUS. WHERE TO NEXT, THEN?
A PLACE CALLED BROWNSVILLE.
WE'VE JUST COME FROM THE LOWER EAST SIDE TO MIDTOWN AND NOW WE'RE BACKTRACKING ALL THE WAY TO BROOKLYN?
WHAT OTH--
BZZT BZZT
OOOH! MY NEW PHONE IS ALREADY RINGING. I CAN DO THAT THING I SAW ON THE INTERNET!
NEW PHONE, WHO DIS?
MERCIFUL HEAVENS.

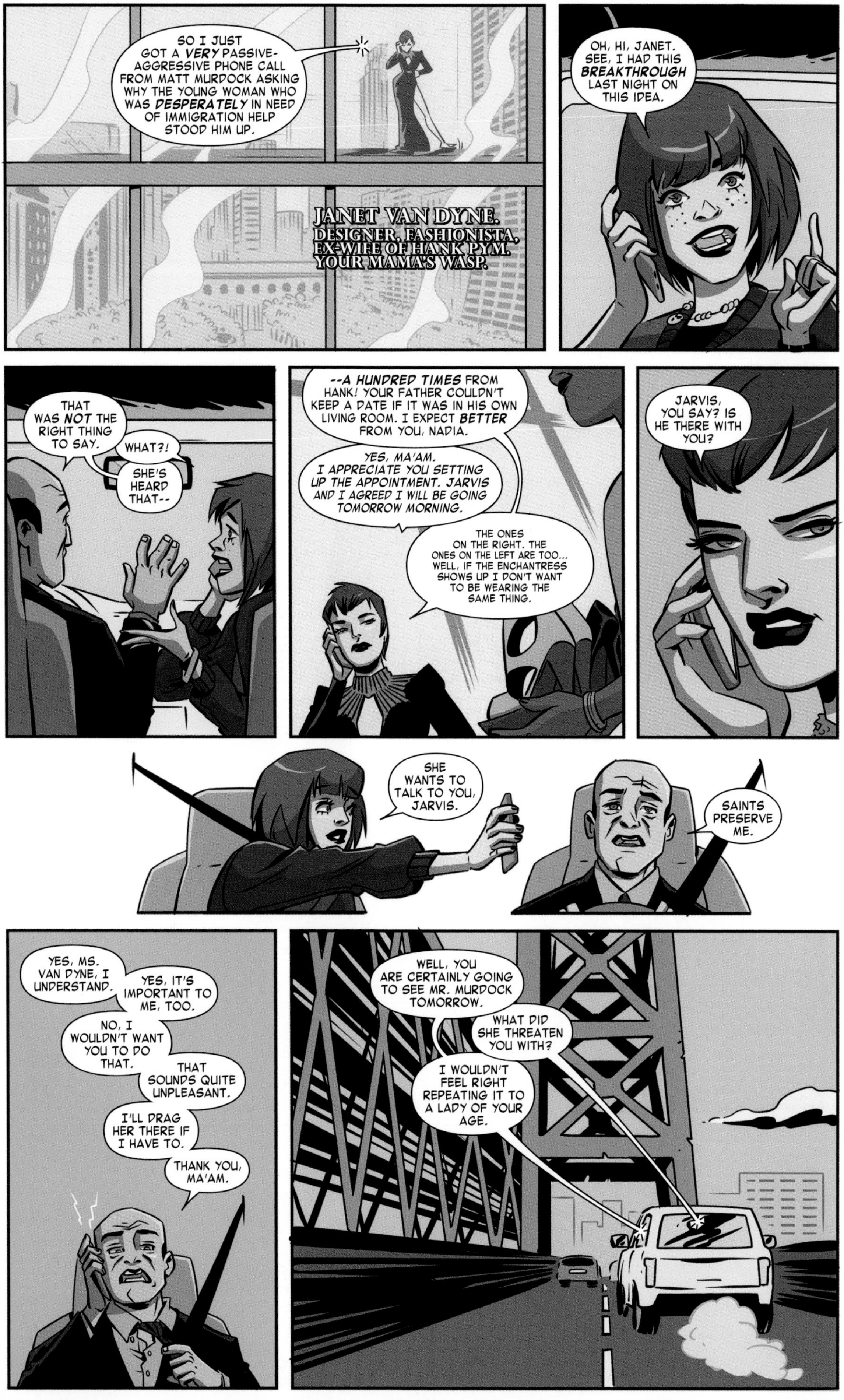

SO I JUST GOT A VERY PASSIVE-AGGRESSIVE PHONE CALL FROM MATT MURDOCK ASKING WHY THE YOUNG WOMAN WHO WAS DESPERATELY IN NEED OF IMMIGRATION HELP STOOD HIM UP.
JANET VAN DYNE. DESIGNER, FASHIONISTA, EX-WIFE OF HANK PYM. YOUR MAMA'S WASP.
OH, HI, JANET. SEE, I HAD THIS BREAKTHROUGH LAST NIGHT ON THIS IDEA.
THAT WAS NOT THE RIGHT THING TO SAY.
WHAT?!
SHE'S HEARD THAT--
--A HUNDRED TIMES FROM HANK! YOUR FATHER COULDN'T KEEP A DATE IF IT WAS IN HIS OWN LIVING ROOM. I EXPECT BETTER FROM YOU, NADIA.
YES, MA'AM. I APPRECIATE YOU SETTING UP THE APPOINTMENT. JARVIS AND I AGREED I WILL BE GOING TOMORROW MORNING.
THE ONES ON THE RIGHT. THE ONES ON THE LEFT ARE TOO... WELL, IF THE ENCHANTRESS SHOWS UP I DON'T WANT TO BE WEARING THE SAME THING.
JARVIS, YOU SAY? IS HE THERE WITH YOU?
SHE WANTS TO TALK TO YOU, JARVIS.
SAINTS PRESERVE ME.
YES, MS. VAN DYNE, I UNDERSTAND.
YES, IT'S IMPORTANT TO ME, TOO.
NO, I WOULDN'T WANT YOU TO DO THAT.
THAT SOUNDS QUITE UNPLEASANT.
I'LL DRAG HER THERE IF I HAVE TO.
THANK YOU, MA'AM.
WELL, YOU ARE CERTAINLY GOING TO SEE MR. MURDOCK TOMORROW.
WHAT DID SHE THREATEN YOU WITH?
I WOULDN'T FEEL RIGHT REPEATING IT TO A LADY OF YOUR AGE.

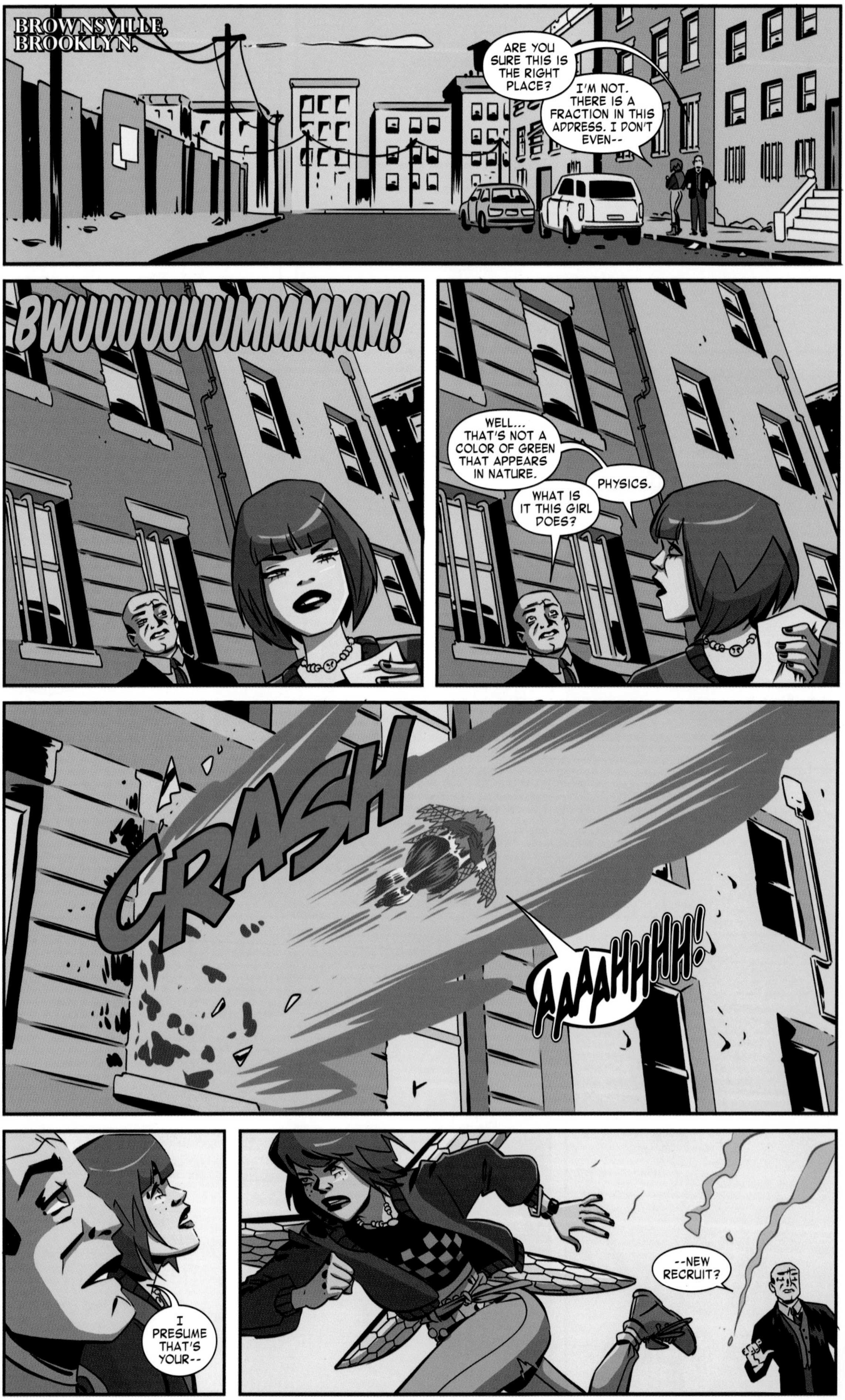
BROWNSVILLE, BROOKLYN.
ARE YOU SURE THIS IS THE RIGHT PLACE?
I'M NOT. THERE IS A FRACTION IN THIS ADDRESS. I DON'T EVEN--
BWUUUUUUUUMMMMMM!
WELL... THAT'S NOT A COLOR OF GREEN THAT APPEARS IN NATURE.
PHYSICS.
WHAT IS IT THIS GIRL DOES?
CRASH
AAAAHHHH!
I PRESUME THAT'S YOUR--
--NEW RECRUIT?

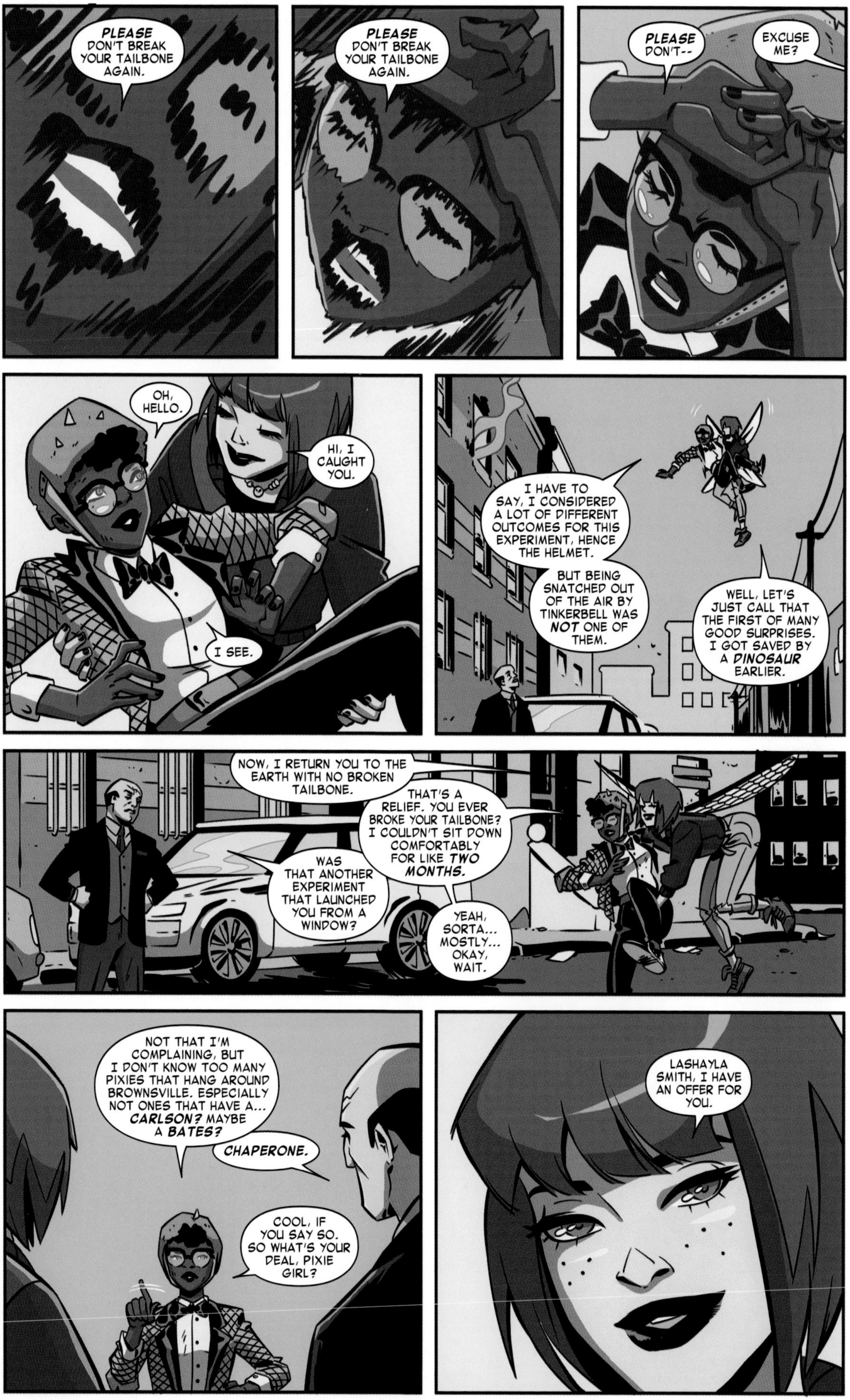
PLEASE DON'T BREAK YOUR TAILBONE AGAIN.
PLEASE DON'T BREAK YOUR TAILBONE AGAIN.
PLEASE DON'T--
EXCUSE ME?
OH, HELLO.
HI, I CAUGHT YOU.
I SEE.
I HAVE TO SAY, I CONSIDERED A LOT OF DIFFERENT OUTCOMES FOR THIS EXPERIMENT, HENCE THE HELMET.
BUT BEING SNATCHED OUT OF THE AIR BY TINKERBELL WAS NOT ONE OF THEM.
WELL, LET'S JUST CALL THAT THE FIRST OF MANY GOOD SURPRISES. I GOT SAVED BY A DINOSAUR EARLIER.
NOW, I RETURN YOU TO THE EARTH WITH NO BROKEN TAILBONE.
THAT'S A RELIEF. YOU EVER BROKE YOUR TAILBONE? I COULDN'T SIT DOWN COMFORTABLY FOR LIKE TWO MONTHS.
WAS THAT ANOTHER EXPERIMENT THAT LAUNCHED YOU FROM A WINDOW?
YEAH, SORTA... MOSTLY... OKAY, WAIT.
NOT THAT I'M COMPLAINING, BUT I DON'T KNOW TOO MANY PIXIES THAT HANG AROUND BROWNSVILLE. ESPECIALLY NOT ONES THAT HAVE A... CARLSON? MAYBE A BATES?
CHAPERONE.
COOL, IF YOU SAY SO. SO WHAT'S YOUR DEAL, PIXIE GIRL?
LASHAYLA SMITH, I HAVE AN OFFER FOR YOU.

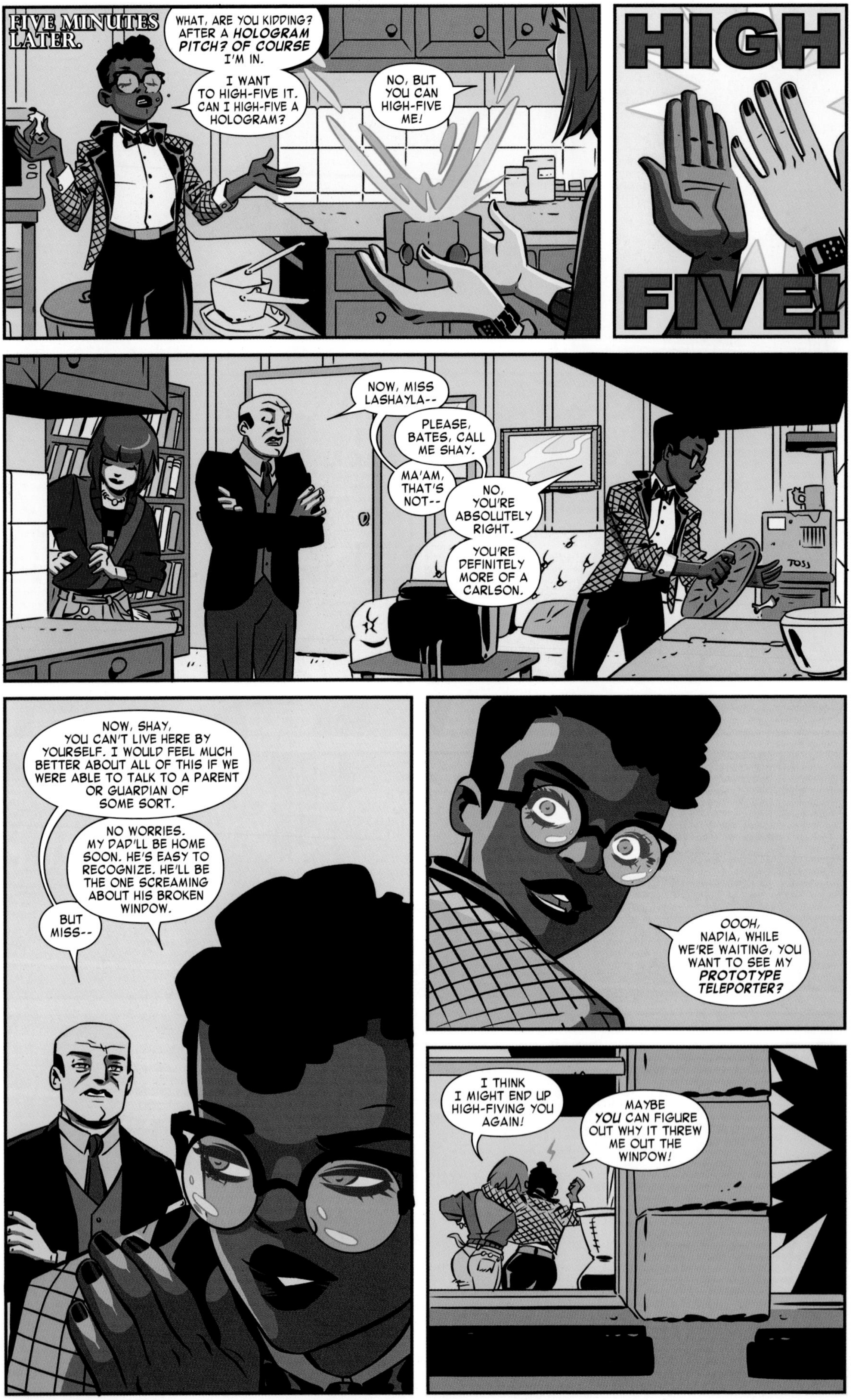
FIVE MINUTES LATER.
WHAT, ARE YOU KIDDING? AFTER A HOLOGRAM PITCH? OF COURSE I'M IN.
I WANT TO HIGH-FIVE IT. CAN I HIGH-FIVE A HOLOGRAM?
NO, BUT YOU CAN HIGH-FIVE ME!
HIGH FIVE!
NOW, MISS LASHAYLA--
PLEASE, BATES, CALL ME SHAY.
MA'AM, THAT'S NOT--
NO, YOU'RE ABSOLUTELY RIGHT.
YOU'RE DEFINITELY MORE OF A CARLSON.
TOSS
NOW, SHAY, YOU CAN'T LIVE HERE BY YOURSELF. I WOULD FEEL MUCH BETTER ABOUT ALL OF THIS IF WE WERE ABLE TO TALK TO A PARENT OR GUARDIAN OF SOME SORT.
NO WORRIES. MY DAD'LL BE HOME SOON. HE'S EASY TO RECOGNIZE. HE'LL BE THE ONE SCREAMING ABOUT HIS BROKEN WINDOW.
BUT MISS--
OOOH, NADIA, WHILE WE'RE WAITING, YOU WANT TO SEE MY PROTOTYPE TELEPORTER?
I THINK I MIGHT END UP HIGH-FIVING YOU AGAIN!
MAYBE YOU CAN FIGURE OUT WHY IT THREW ME OUT THE WINDOW!

WOW, THIS IS BRILLIANT. WHAT MADE YOU DECIDE TO BUILD A PORTAL?

YOU EVER HAVE AN *EPIPHANY*, NADIA? LIKE, YOU'RE THINKING ABOUT ALL YOUR PROBLEMS AND YOU REALIZE THERE'S ONE SOLUTION?

JUST ONCE.

A FEW MONTHS AGO, I GOT PRETTY DEPRESSED. I STOPPED GETTING OUT OF BED. I STARTED SKIPPING SCHOOL, EVEN THOUGH I *LOVED* SCHOOL.

WHY?

FIRST, MOM HAD TO MOVE FOR HER JOB, BUT DAD COULDN'T LEAVE HIS. NOW I NEVER SEE HER. DAD WORKS LONG HOURS AND HAS A LONG COMMUTE, SO I'M ALONE A LOT. THEN THESE GIRLS STARTED BEATING ME UP ON THE WAY HOME.

THAT MUST HAVE BEEN HARD.

IT WAS. BUT MY FOURTH DAY OF LYING IN BED, I HAD A THOUGHT.

WHAT IF I COULD BE AT MOM'S *RIGHT NOW?* WHAT IF DAD COULD GET HOME THE MOMENT WORK WAS DONE? WHAT IF I *DIDN'T* HAVE TO WALK HOME ALONE?

TELEPORTER.

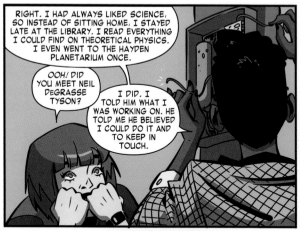

RIGHT. I HAD ALWAYS LIKED SCIENCE, SO INSTEAD OF SITTING HOME, I STAYED LATE AT THE LIBRARY. I READ EVERYTHING I COULD FIND ON THEORETICAL PHYSICS. I EVEN WENT TO THE HAYDEN PLANETARIUM ONCE.

OOH! DID YOU MEET NEIL DEGRASSE TYSON?

I DID. I TOLD HIM WHAT I WAS WORKING ON. HE TOLD ME HE BELIEVED I COULD DO IT AND TO KEEP IN TOUCH.

DID YOU? DID YOU KEEP IN TOUCH?

NEVER. NOT UNTIL I GET THIS THING WORKING.

BUT HE COULD--

I WANT HIM TO KNOW HE WAS RIGHT ABOUT ME. I WANT--

PRICILLA LASHAYLA SMITH! WHAT DID YOU DO TO MY APARTMENT?

WELL, HERE THIS COMES.

DON'T WORRY, I GOT IT!

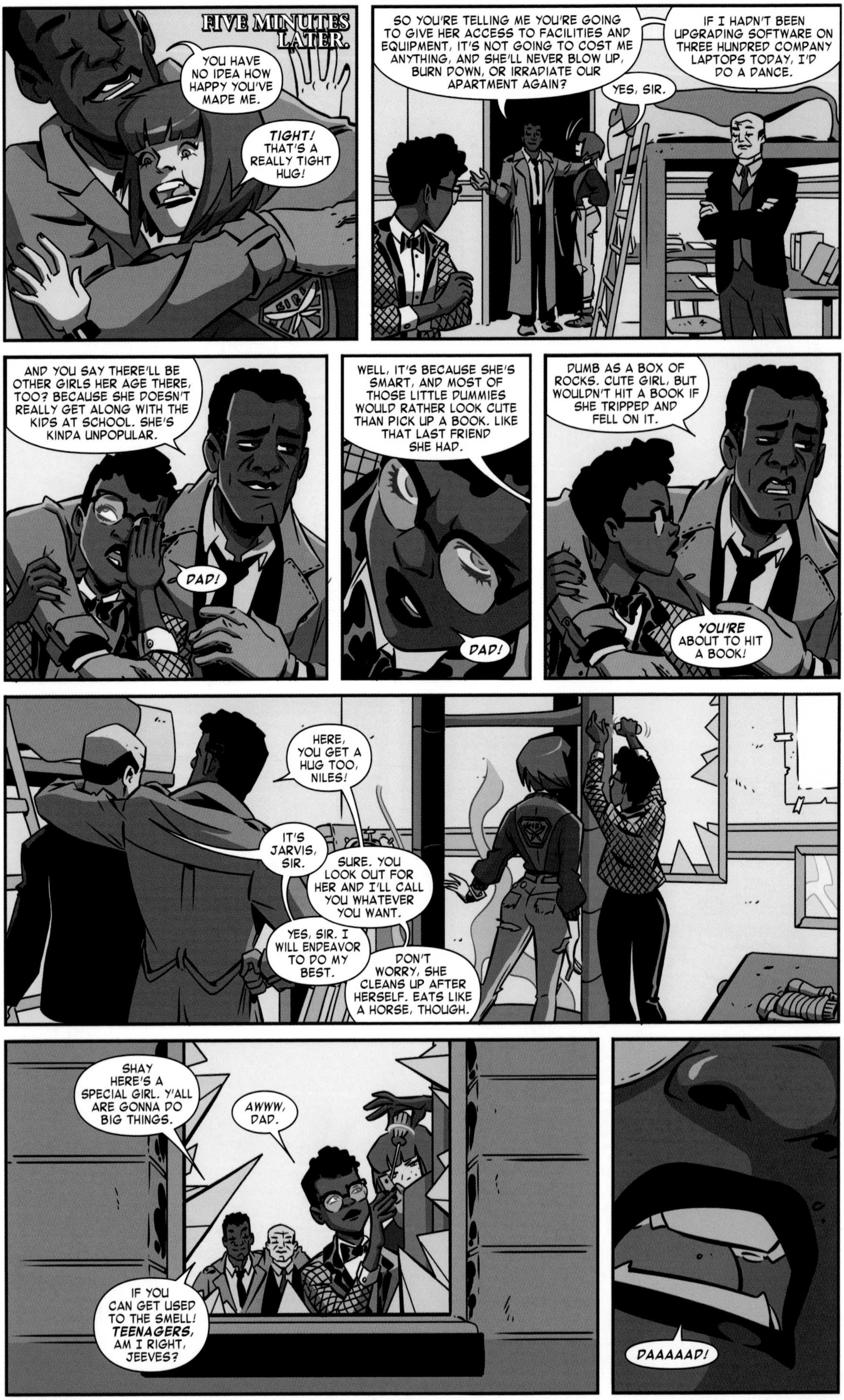
FIVE MINUTES LATER.
YOU HAVE NO IDEA HOW HAPPY YOU'VE MADE ME.
TIGHT! THAT'S A REALLY TIGHT HUG!
SO YOU'RE TELLING ME YOU'RE GOING TO GIVE HER ACCESS TO FACILITIES AND EQUIPMENT, IT'S NOT GOING TO COST ME ANYTHING, AND SHE'LL NEVER BLOW UP, BURN DOWN, OR IRRADIATE OUR APARTMENT AGAIN?
YES, SIR.
IF I HADN'T BEEN UPGRADING SOFTWARE ON THREE HUNDRED COMPANY LAPTOPS TODAY, I'D DO A DANCE.
AND YOU SAY THERE'LL BE OTHER GIRLS HER AGE THERE, TOO? BECAUSE SHE DOESN'T REALLY GET ALONG WITH THE KIDS AT SCHOOL. SHE'S KINDA UNPOPULAR.
DAD!
WELL, IT'S BECAUSE SHE'S SMART, AND MOST OF THOSE LITTLE DUMMIES WOULD RATHER LOOK CUTE THAN PICK UP A BOOK. LIKE THAT LAST FRIEND SHE HAD.
DAD!
DUMB AS A BOX OF ROCKS. CUTE GIRL, BUT WOULDN'T HIT A BOOK IF SHE TRIPPED AND FELL ON IT.
YOU'RE ABOUT TO HIT A BOOK!
HERE, YOU GET A HUG TOO, NILES!
IT'S JARVIS, SIR.
SURE. YOU LOOK OUT FOR HER AND I'LL CALL YOU WHATEVER YOU WANT.
YES, SIR. I WILL ENDEAVOR TO DO MY BEST.
DON'T WORRY, SHE CLEANS UP AFTER HERSELF. EATS LIKE A HORSE, THOUGH.
SHAY HERE'S A SPECIAL GIRL. Y'ALL ARE GONNA DO BIG THINGS.
AWWW, DAD.
IF YOU CAN GET USED TO THE SMELL! TEENAGERS, AM I RIGHT, JEEVES?
DAAAAAD!

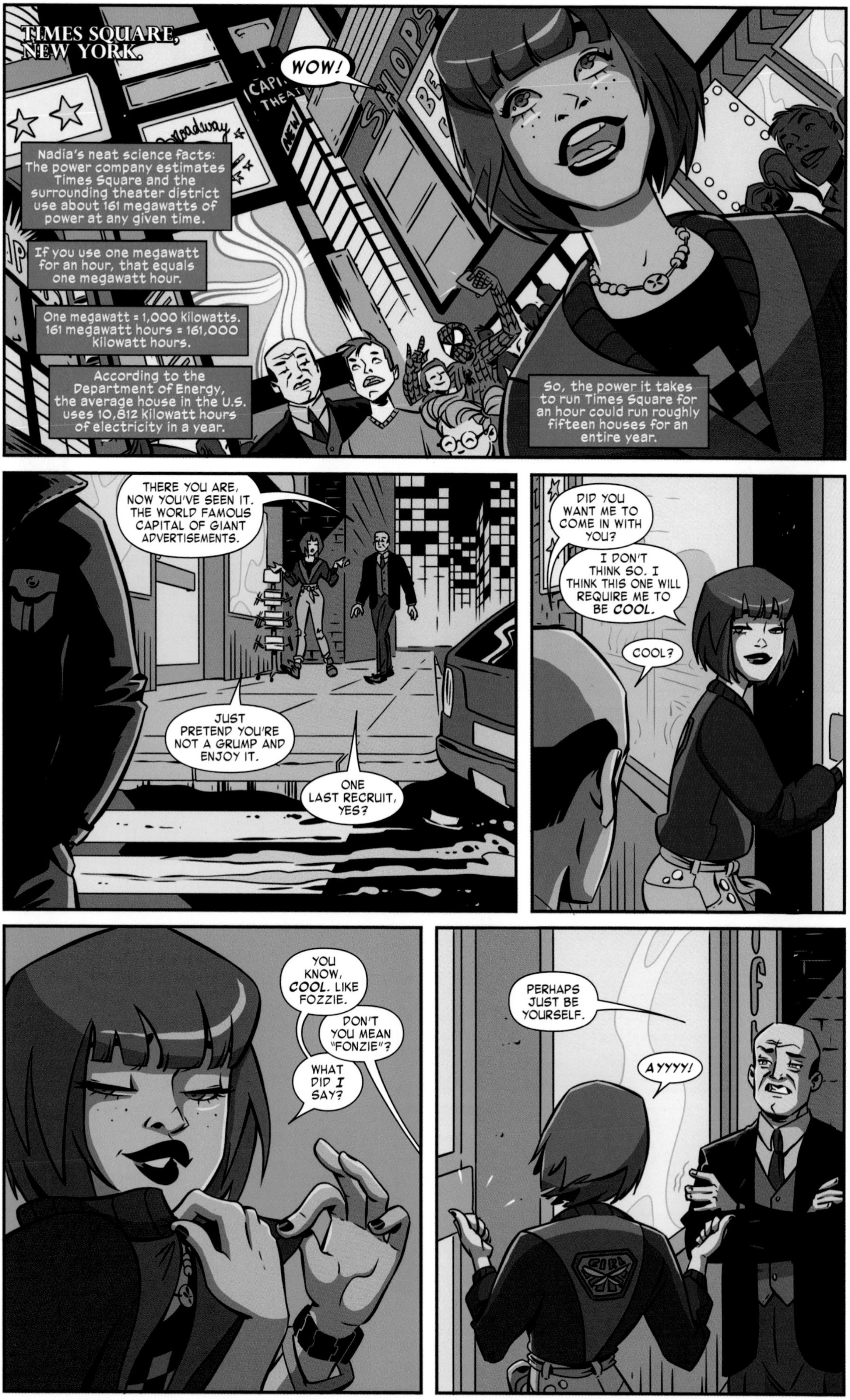
TIMES SQUARE, NEW YORK.
WOW!
CAPI THEAT
SHOPS
NEW
Broadway
Nadia's neat science facts: The power company estimates Times Square and the surrounding theater district use about 161 megawatts of power at any given time.
If you use one megawatt for an hour, that equals one megawatt hour.
One megawatt = 1,000 kilowatts. 161 megawatt hours = 161,000 kilowatt hours.
According to the Department of Energy, the average house in the U.S. uses 10,812 kilowatt hours of electricity in a year.
So, the power it takes to run Times Square for an hour could run roughly fifteen houses for an entire year.
THERE YOU ARE, NOW YOU'VE SEEN IT. THE WORLD FAMOUS CAPITAL OF GIANT ADVERTISEMENTS.
JUST PRETEND YOU'RE NOT A GRUMP AND ENJOY IT.
ONE LAST RECRUIT, YES?
DID YOU WANT ME TO COME IN WITH YOU?
I DON'T THINK SO. I THINK THIS ONE WILL REQUIRE ME TO BE COOL.
COOL?
YOU KNOW, COOL. LIKE FOZZIE.
DON'T YOU MEAN "FONZIE"?
WHAT DID I SAY?
PERHAPS JUST BE YOURSELF.
AYYYY!

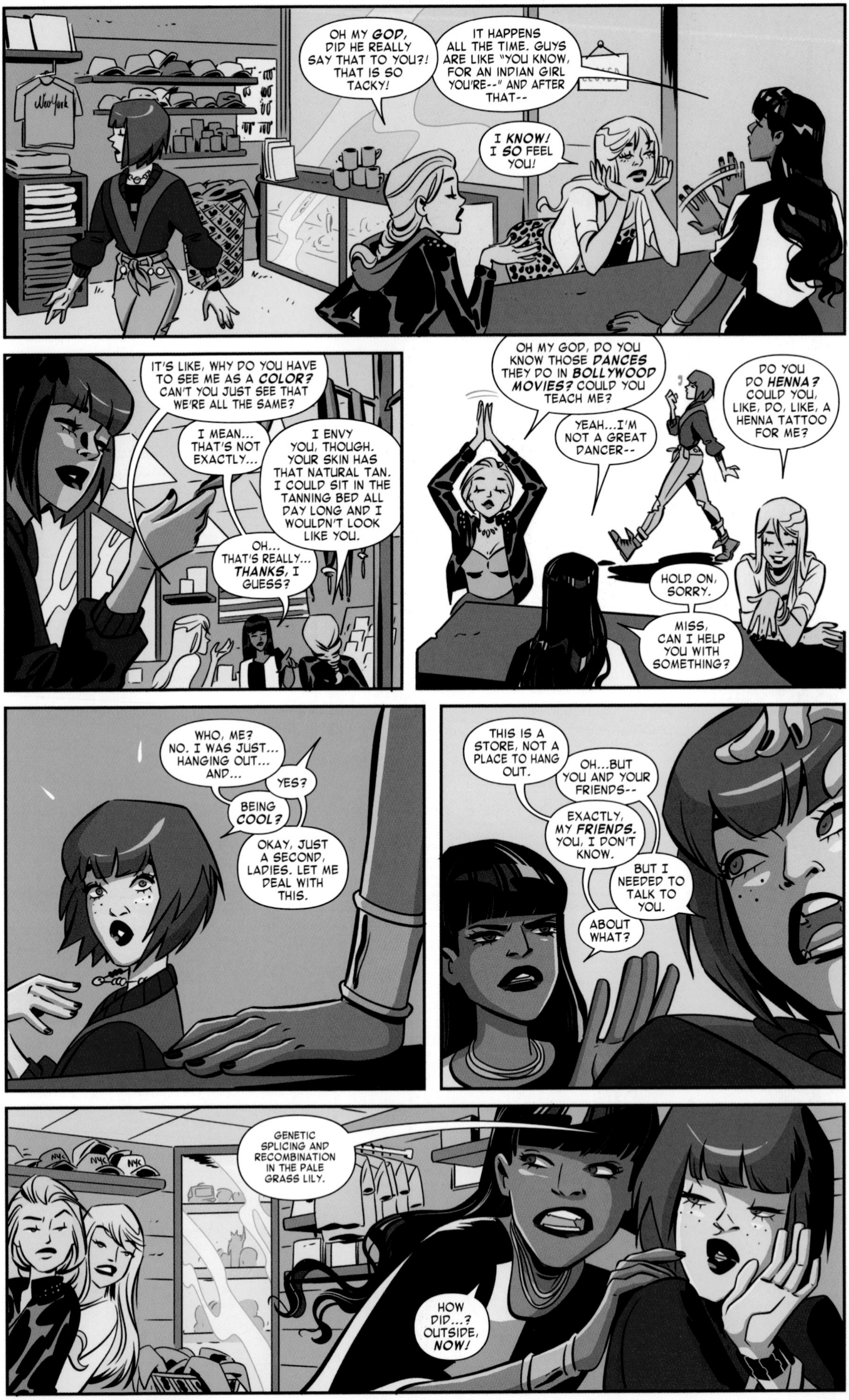
OH MY GOD, DID HE REALLY SAY THAT TO YOU?! THAT IS SO TACKY!
IT HAPPENS ALL THE TIME. GUYS ARE LIKE "YOU KNOW, FOR AN INDIAN GIRL YOU'RE--" AND AFTER THAT--
I KNOW! I SO FEEL YOU!
IT'S LIKE, WHY DO YOU HAVE TO SEE ME AS A COLOR? CAN'T YOU JUST SEE THAT WE'RE ALL THE SAME?
I MEAN... THAT'S NOT EXACTLY...
I ENVY YOU, THOUGH. YOUR SKIN HAS THAT NATURAL TAN. I COULD SIT IN THE TANNING BED ALL DAY LONG AND I WOULDN'T LOOK LIKE YOU.
OH... THAT'S REALLY... THANKS, I GUESS?
OH MY GOD, DO YOU KNOW THOSE DANCES THEY DO IN BOLLYWOOD MOVIES? COULD YOU TEACH ME?
YEAH...I'M NOT A GREAT DANCER--
DO YOU DO HENNA? COULD YOU, LIKE, DO, LIKE, A HENNA TATTOO FOR ME?
HOLD ON, SORRY.
MISS, CAN I HELP YOU WITH SOMETHING?
WHO, ME? NO. I WAS JUST... HANGING OUT... AND...
YES?
BEING COOL?
OKAY, JUST A SECOND, LADIES. LET ME DEAL WITH THIS.
THIS IS A STORE, NOT A PLACE TO HANG OUT.
OH...BUT YOU AND YOUR FRIENDS--
EXACTLY, MY FRIENDS. YOU, I DON'T KNOW.
BUT I NEEDED TO TALK TO YOU.
ABOUT WHAT?
GENETIC SPLICING AND RECOMBINATION IN THE PALE GRASS LILY.
HOW DID...? OUTSIDE, NOW!

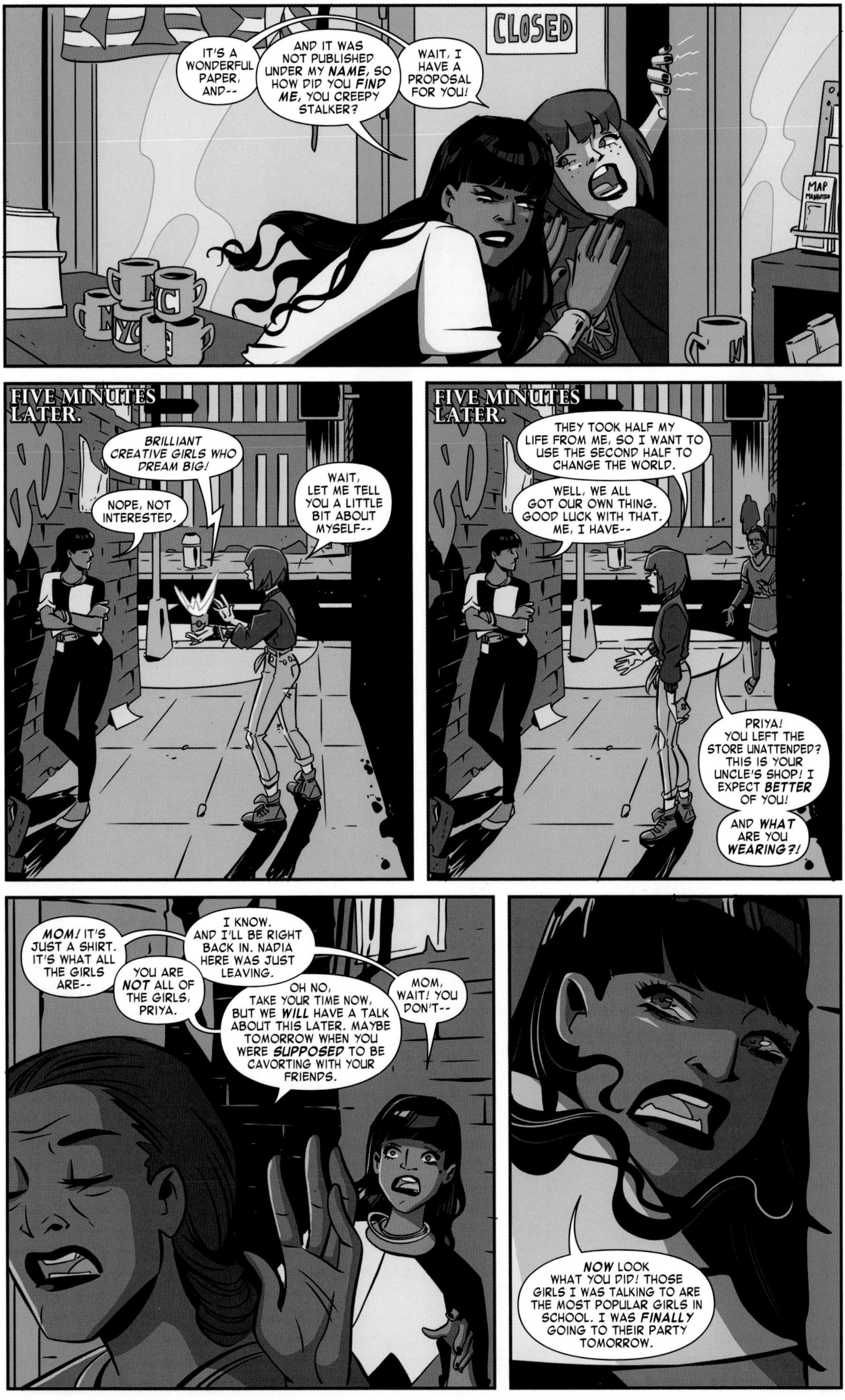

CLOSED
IT'S A WONDERFUL PAPER, AND--
AND IT WAS NOT PUBLISHED UNDER MY NAME, SO HOW DID YOU FIND ME, YOU CREEPY STALKER?
WAIT, I HAVE A PROPOSAL FOR YOU!
MAP
FIVE MINUTES LATER.
BRILLIANT CREATIVE GIRLS WHO DREAM BIG!
NOPE, NOT INTERESTED.
WAIT, LET ME TELL YOU A LITTLE BIT ABOUT MYSELF--
FIVE MINUTES LATER.
THEY TOOK HALF MY LIFE FROM ME, SO I WANT TO USE THE SECOND HALF TO CHANGE THE WORLD.
WELL, WE ALL GOT OUR OWN THING. GOOD LUCK WITH THAT. ME, I HAVE--
PRIYA! YOU LEFT THE STORE UNATTENDED? THIS IS YOUR UNCLE'S SHOP! I EXPECT BETTER OF YOU!
AND WHAT ARE YOU WEARING?!
MOM! IT'S JUST A SHIRT. IT'S WHAT ALL THE GIRLS ARE--
YOU ARE NOT ALL OF THE GIRLS, PRIYA.
I KNOW. AND I'LL BE RIGHT BACK IN. NADIA HERE WAS JUST LEAVING.
OH NO, TAKE YOUR TIME NOW, BUT WE WILL HAVE A TALK ABOUT THIS LATER. MAYBE TOMORROW WHEN YOU WERE SUPPOSED TO BE CAVORTING WITH YOUR FRIENDS.
MOM, WAIT! YOU DON'T--
NOW LOOK WHAT YOU DID! THOSE GIRLS I WAS TALKING TO ARE THE MOST POPULAR GIRLS IN SCHOOL. I WAS FINALLY GOING TO THEIR PARTY TOMORROW.

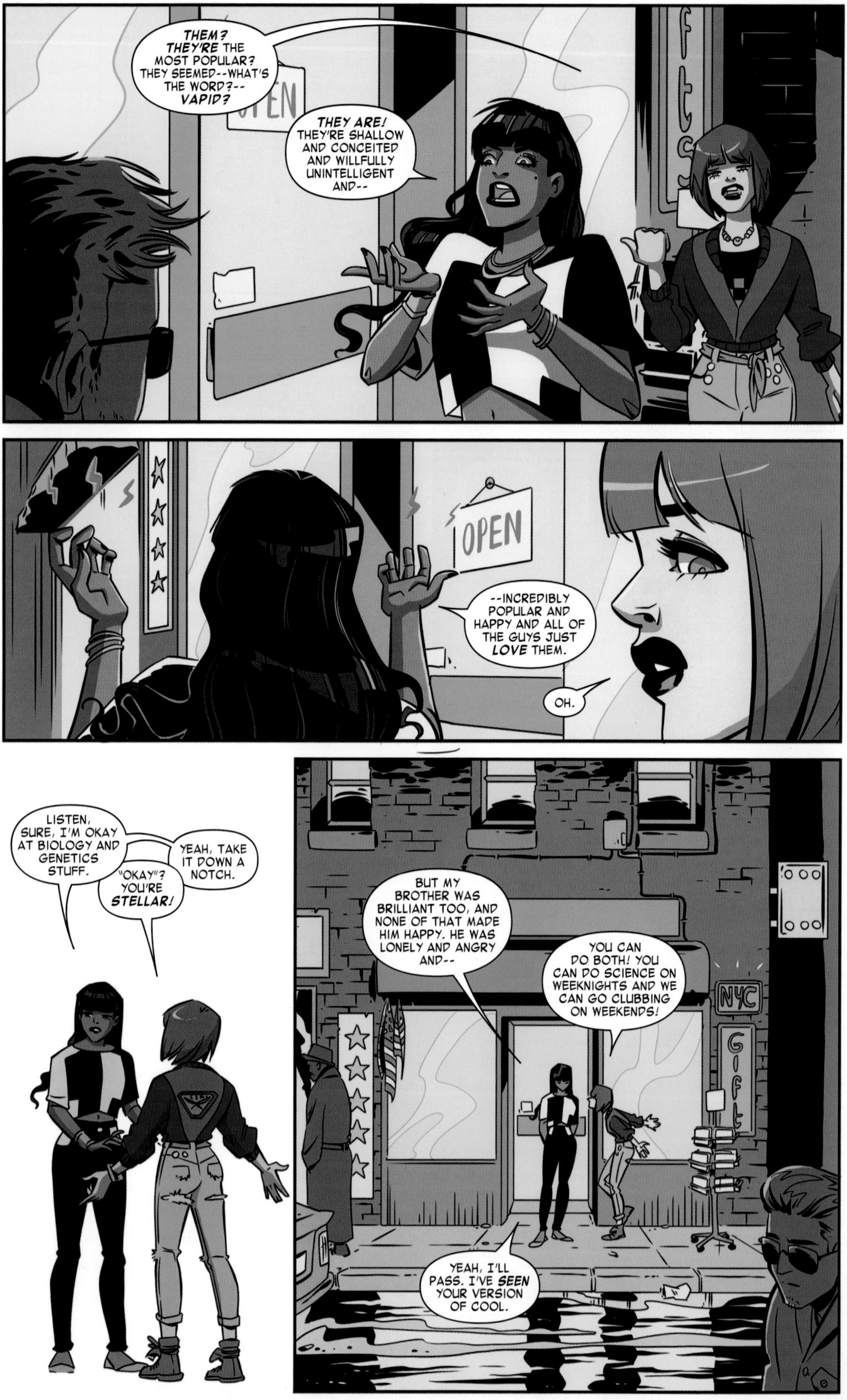
THEM? THEY'RE THE MOST POPULAR? THEY SEEMED--WHAT'S THE WORD?--VAPID?
OPEN
THEY ARE! THEY'RE SHALLOW AND CONCEITED AND WILLFULLY UNINTELLIGENT AND--
OPEN
--INCREDIBLY POPULAR AND HAPPY AND ALL OF THE GUYS JUST LOVE THEM.
OH.
LISTEN, SURE, I'M OKAY AT BIOLOGY AND GENETICS STUFF.
"OKAY"? YOU'RE STELLAR!
YEAH, TAKE IT DOWN A NOTCH.
BUT MY BROTHER WAS BRILLIANT TOO, AND NONE OF THAT MADE HIM HAPPY. HE WAS LONELY AND ANGRY AND--
YOU CAN DO BOTH! YOU CAN DO SCIENCE ON WEEKNIGHTS AND WE CAN GO CLUBBING ON WEEKENDS!
NYC
GIFT
YEAH, I'LL PASS. I'VE SEEN YOUR VERSION OF COOL.

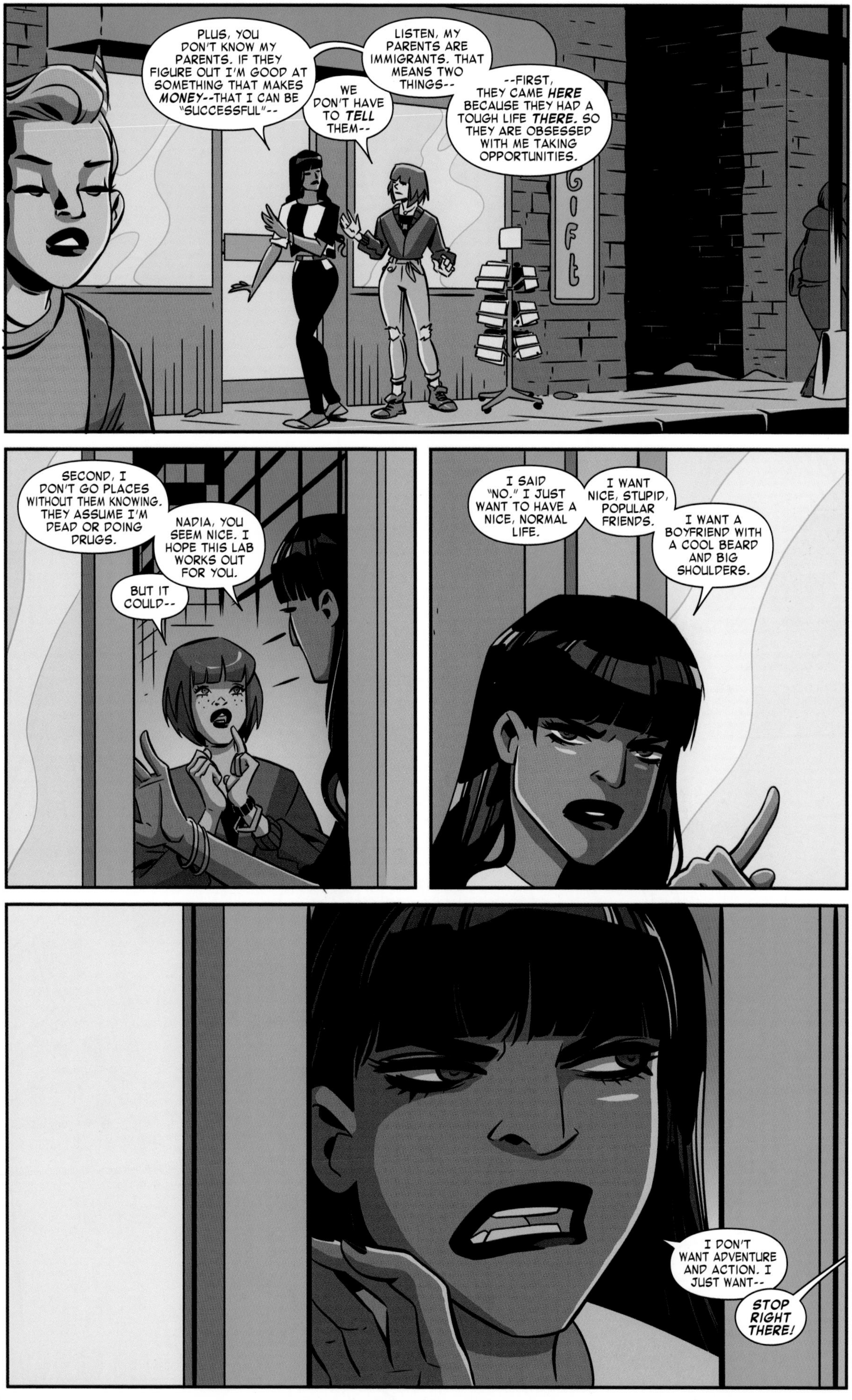
PLUS, YOU DON'T KNOW MY PARENTS. IF THEY FIGURE OUT I'M GOOD AT SOMETHING THAT MAKES MONEY--THAT I CAN BE "SUCCESSFUL"--
WE DON'T HAVE TO TELL THEM--
LISTEN, MY PARENTS ARE IMMIGRANTS. THAT MEANS TWO THINGS--
--FIRST, THEY CAME HERE BECAUSE THEY HAD A TOUGH LIFE THERE. SO THEY ARE OBSESSED WITH ME TAKING OPPORTUNITIES.
GIFT
SECOND, I DON'T GO PLACES WITHOUT THEM KNOWING. THEY ASSUME I'M DEAD OR DOING DRUGS.
NADIA, YOU SEEM NICE. I HOPE THIS LAB WORKS OUT FOR YOU.
BUT IT COULD--
I SAID "NO." I JUST WANT TO HAVE A NICE, NORMAL LIFE.
I WANT NICE, STUPID, POPULAR FRIENDS.
I WANT A BOYFRIEND WITH A COOL BEARD AND BIG SHOULDERS.
I DON'T WANT ADVENTURE AND ACTION. I JUST WANT--
STOP RIGHT THERE!

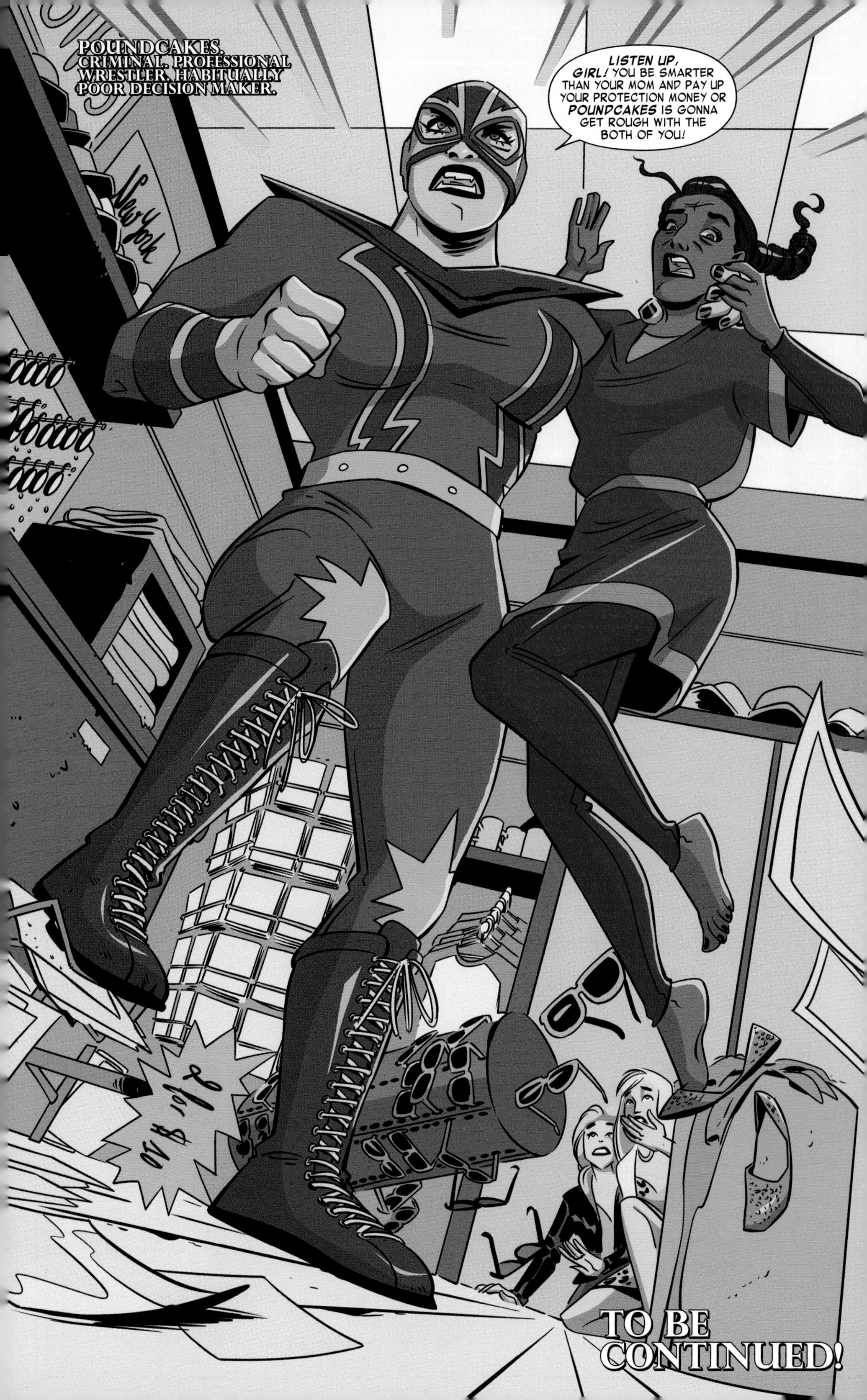
POUNDCAKES. CRIMINAL. PROFESSIONAL WRESTLER. HABITUALLY POOR DECISION MAKER.
LISTEN UP, GIRL! YOU BE SMARTER THAN YOUR MOM AND PAY UP YOUR PROTECTION MONEY OR POUNDCAKES IS GONNA GET ROUGH WITH THE BOTH OF YOU!
TO BE CONTINUED!

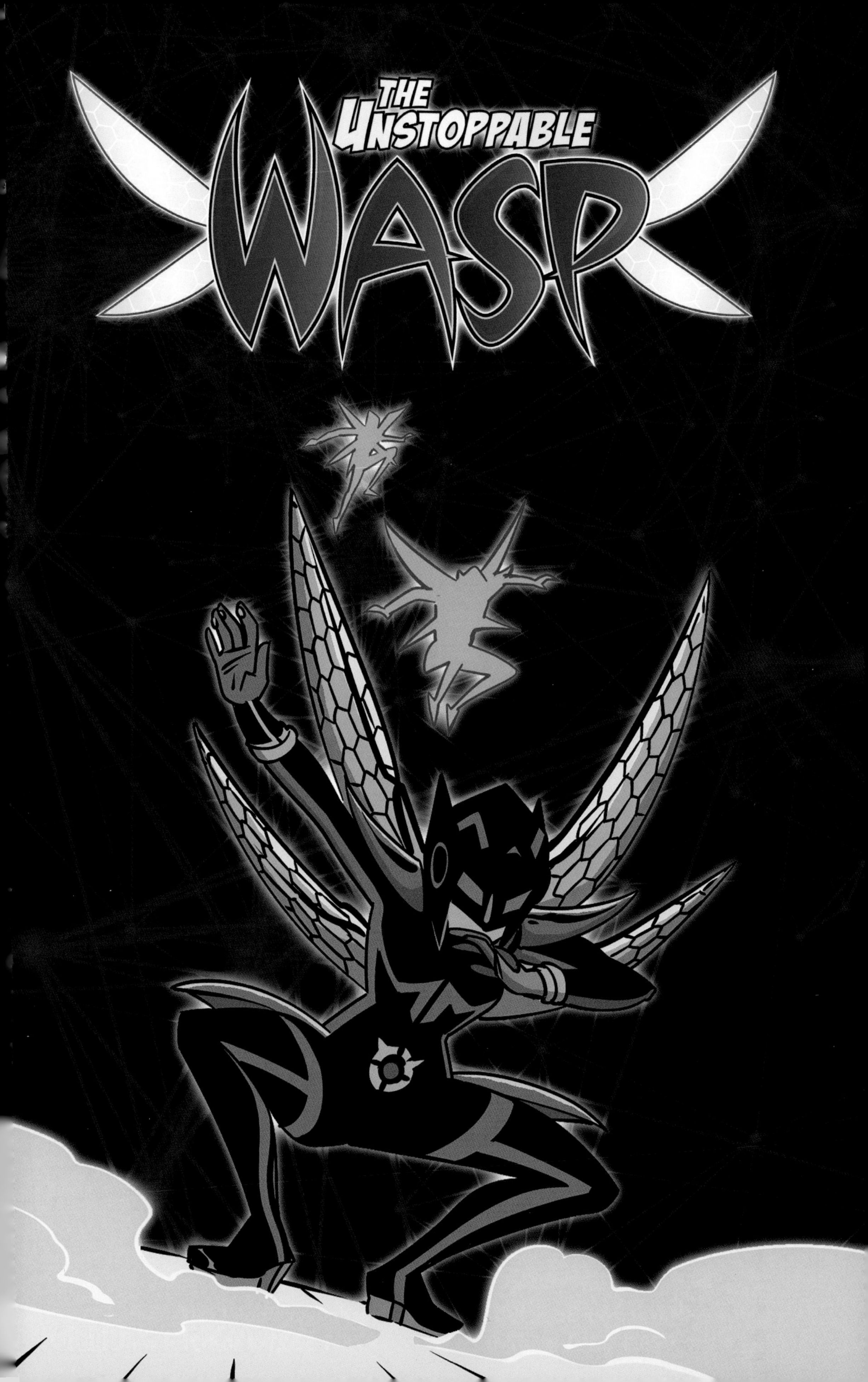
THE UNSTOPPABLE
WASP

THE UNSTOPPABLE WASP

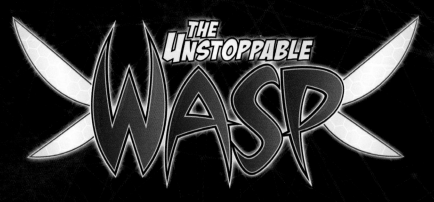

COLLECT THEM ALL!

Set of 4 Hardcover Books ISBN: 978-1-5321-4364-9

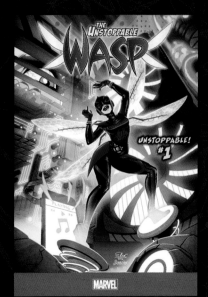

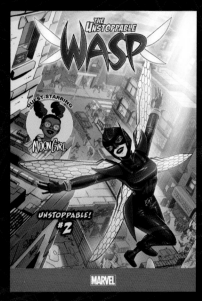

THE UNSTOPPABLE
WASP
UNSTOPPABLE! #1
MARVEL

Hardcover Book ISBN
978-1-5321-4365-6

THE UNSTOPPABLE
WASP
GUEST-STARRING
MOON GIRL
UNSTOPPABLE! #2
MARVEL

Hardcover Book ISBN
978-1-5321-4366-3

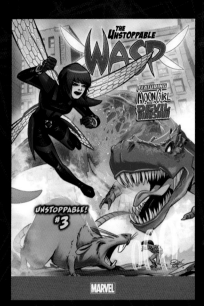

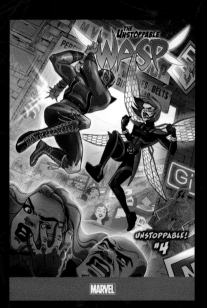

THE UNSTOPPABLE
WASP
FEATURING
MOON GIRL
DEVIL DINOSAUR
UNSTOPPABLE! #3
MARVEL

Hardcover Book ISBN
978-1-5321-4367-0

THE UNSTOPPABLE
WASP
UNSTOPPABLE! #4
MARVEL

Hardcover Book ISBN
978-1-5321-4368-7